FAI

MS WIZ

PRAISE FOR THE MS WIZ BOOKS:

'Funny, magical ... with wicked pictures
by Tony Ross, it's the closest thing you'll
get to Roald Dahl'
The Times

'Wonderfully funny and exciting'
Books for Keeps

'Ms Wiz is everyone's favourite'
Young Calibre Library

'Hilarious and hysterical'
Sunday Times

'The fantastic Ms Wiz books'
Malorie Blackman

TERENCE BLACKER

FANGTASTIC, Ms Wiz

Illustrated by
TONY ROSS

ANDERSEN PRESS
LONDON

First published in Great Britain in 2008 by
ANDERSEN PRESS LIMITED
20 Vauxhall Bridge Road
London SW1V 2SA
www.andersenpress.co.uk

Ms Wiz Spells Trouble first published in 1988 by Piccadilly Press Limited
Ms Wiz Loves Dracula first published in 1993 by Piccadilly Press Limited

British Library Cataloguing in Publication Data available.

ISBN 978 184 270 703 6

Typeset by FiSH Books, Enfield, Middx.
Printed and bound in Great Britain by CPI Bookmarque, Croydon, Surrey

Ms Wiz

Ms Wiz

Ms Wiz

SPELLS TROUBLE

For Alice

CHAPTER ONE
A NEW ARRIVAL

Most teachers are strange and the teachers at St Barnabas School were no exception.

Yet it's almost certain that none of them – not Mr Gilbert, the head teacher, who liked to pick his nose during Assembly, not Mrs Hicks who talked to her teddies in class, not Miss Gomaz who smoked cigarettes in the lavatory – *none* of them was quite as odd as Class Five's new teacher.

Some of the children in Class Five thought she was a witch. Others said she was a hippy. A few of them thought she was just a bit mad. But they all agreed that there had never been anyone quite like her at St Barnabas before.

This is her story. I wonder what *you* think she was...

As soon as their new teacher walked into the classroom on the first day of term, the children of Class Five sensed that there was something different about her. She was quite tall, with long black hair and bright green eyes. She wore tight jeans and a purple blouse. Her fingers were decorated with several large rings and black nail varnish. She looked as if she were on her way to a disco, not teaching at a school.

Most surprising of all, she wasn't frightened. Class Five was known in the school as the "problem class". It had a

reputation for being difficult and noisy, for having what was called a"disruptive element". Miss Jones, their last teacher, had left the school in tears. But none of that seemed to worry this strange-looking new teacher.

"My name is Miss Wisdom," she said in a quiet but firm voice. "So what do you say to me every morning when I walk in?"

"Good morning, Miss Wisdom," said Class Five unenthusiastically.

"Wrong," said the teacher with a flash of her green eyes, "You say 'Hi, Ms Wiz!' "

Jack, who was one of Class Five's Disruptive Element, giggled at the back of the class.

"Yo," he said in a silly American accent. "Why, hi Ms Wiz!"

Caroline, the class dreamer, was paying attention for a change.

"Why is it Ms...er, Ms?" she asked.

"Well," said Ms Wiz, "I'm not a Mrs because I'm not married, thank goodness, and I'm not Miss because I think Miss sounds silly for a grown woman, don't you?"

"Not as silly as Ms," muttered Katrina, who liked to find fault wherever possible.

"And why Wiz?" asked a rather large boy sitting in the front row. It was Podge, who was probably the most annoying and certainly the greediest boy in the class.

"Wiz?" said Ms Wiz with a mysterious smile. "Just you wait and see."

Ms Wiz reached inside a big leather

bag that she had placed beside her desk. She pulled out a china cat.

"That," she said, placing the cat carefully on her desk," is my friend Hecate the Cat. She's watching you all the time. She sees everything and hears everything. She's my spy."

Ms Wiz turned to the blackboard.

"Weird," muttered Jack.

An odd, hissing sound came from the china cat. Its eyes lit up like torches.

"Hecate sees you even when my back is turned," said Ms Wiz, who now faced the class. "Will the person who said 'weird' spell it please?"

Everyone stared at Jack,who blushed.

"I.T.," he stammered.

No one laughed.

"Er, W...I..."

"Wrong," said Ms Wiz. "W.E.I.R.D. If you don't know how to spell a word, Jack, don't use it." She patted the china cat.

"Good girl, Hecate," she said.

"How did she know my name?" whispered Jack.

The new teacher smiled."Children, remember one thing. Ms Wiz knows everything."

"Now," she said briskly. "Pay attention, please. Talking of spelling,

I'm going to give you a first lesson in casting spells."

"Oh great," said Katrina grumpily. "Now we've got a witch for a teacher."

Hecate the Cat hissed angrily.

"No, Katrina, not a witch," said Ms Wiz sharply. "We don't call them

witches these days. It gives people the wrong idea. We call them Paranormal Operatives. Now – any suggestions for our first spell?"

Podge put up his hand immediately.

"Could we turn our crayons into lollipops, please Ms?" he asked.

"No," said Ms Wiz. "Spells are not for personal greed."

"How about turning Class Two into frogs?" asked Katrina.

"Nor are they for revenge. There will be no unpleasant spells around here while I'm your teacher," said Ms Wiz before adding, almost as an afterthought, "unless they're deserved, of course."

She looked out of the window. In the playground Mr Brown, the school caretaker, was sweeping up leaves.

"Please draw the playground," said Ms Wiz. "Imagine it without any leaves. The best picture will create the spell."

Almost for the first time in living memory, Class Five worked in complete quiet. Katrina didn't complain that someone had nicked her pencil. Caroline managed to concentrate on her work. Podge forgot to look in his trouser pocket for one last sweet. Not a single paper pellet was shot across the room by Jack.

At the end of the lesson, Ms Wiz looked at the drawings carefully.

"Well, they're all quite good," she said eventually. "But I think I like Caroline's the best."

She took Caroline's drawing and carefully taped it to the window.

"Please close your eyes while I cast the spell," she said.

There was a curious humming noise as Class Five sat, eyes closed, in silence.

"Open," said Ms Wiz, after a few seconds. "Regard Caroline's work."

The children looked at Caroline's drawing. It was steaming slightly and, in one corner, there was a freshly drawn pile of leaves.

"Hey – look at the playground!" shouted Katrina.

Everyone looked out of the window. To their amazement, the leaves on the ground had disappeared. Mr Brown stood by his wheelbarrow, scratching his head.

"Weird," said Jack. "Very weird indeed."

CHAPTER TWO
"MS WIZ IS MAGIC"

"Yes, I'm afraid she is a bit odd," sighed the head teacher, Mr Gilbert, as he took tea one morning with Miss Gomaz and Mrs Hicks in the Staff Common Room.

"Those jeans," sniffed Miss Gomaz. "And I never thought I'd live to see *black* nail-varnish at St Barnabas."

"But you have to admit she seems to have Class Five under control," said Mr Gilbert. "That's a whole week she's been here and not one child has been sent to my study. Not one window has been broken."

Mrs Hicks stirred her tea disapprovingly.

"It won't last," she said. "The Disruptive Element will get the better of her. And there are some very strange noises coming from that classroom."

"I'd keep an eye on the situation if I were you, head teacher," said Miss Gomaz.

Mr Gilbert sighed.

"Yes," he said wearily. "That's what I'll do. Keep an eye on the situation."

The fact is that Class Five, including the Disruptive Element, were having the time of their lives. Every lesson with Ms Wiz was different.

"Now, Class Five," she would say, "I'm going to teach you something rather unusual. But remember – what happens in this classroom is our secret. The magic only works if nobody except us knows about it."

Surprisingly, Class Five agreed.

So no one– not even parents or other children at the school – had any idea of the strange things that happened to Class Five.

They never heard how Caroline's picture of the playground saved Mr Brown a morning's work.

They never heard how Jack's desk moved to the front of the class all by itself when Hecate spotted him talking at the back.

They never heard how Katrina flew around the class five times on a vacuum cleaner after she had complained that Ms Wiz couldn't be a real witch –sorry, Paranormal Operative – because she didn't ride a broomstick.

They never heard about the nature lesson when the class met Herbert, a

pet rat that Ms Wiz kept up her sleeve.

But they did hear about the day when Podge became the hero of the class.

Nobody could keep *that* a secret.

Once every term, Class Five played a football match against a team from a school nearby, called Brackenhurst. It was a very important game and everyone from St Barnabas gathered in the playground to watch. Last term, Class Five had lost 10–0.

"That was because Miss Jones picked all the wimps," explained Jack.

"Because she was a wimp herself," said Caroline.

The rest of the class agreed noisily.

"*I'll* be manager," shouted Jack over the din.

Ms Wiz held up her hands like a wizard about to cast a spell.

"I'll be manager," she said firmly.

"But you don't know anything about football," said Jack.

"Ms Wiz knows everything," said Caroline.

"Creep!" muttered Katrina.

Hecate the Cat hissed angrily.

"All right, Hecate," said Katrina quickly. "I take it back."

"My team," said Ms Wiz, "is Jack, Simon, Katrina, Alex and..."

She looked around the classroom and saw Podge's arm waving wildly.

"*No*, Ms Wiz," several of the class shouted at once. "Not Podge! He's useless!"

"...and Podge."

There was a groan from around the classroom.

"Here comes another hammering," said Jack gloomily.

For a while during the game that afternoon, it looked as though Jack's prediction had been right. After three minutes, Brackenhurst had already scored twice. Podge had been a disaster, falling over his own feet every time the ball came near him.

"Serves that Ms Cleverclogs right," said Mrs Hicks, who was watching the match with Miss Gomaz. "Look at her, jumping up and down like that, making herself look foolish in front of the kiddies. Anybody would think she was a child herself."

"It's embarrassing, that's what it is," agreed Miss Gomaz.

"*Do* something," said Caroline who was standing next to Ms Wiz.

"And what do you suggest, Caroline?" asked Ms Wiz whose normally pale face was now quite red.

"You know," whispered Caroline. "Something *special*."

"Oh, all right," sighed Ms Wiz. "I suppose a *little* magic wouldn't hurt."

At that moment, Podge blundered into one of the Brackenhurst's players and knocked him over. Mr Gilbert, who was referee, blew hard on his whistle for a free kick against Class Five – but not a sound came out. In fact, the only sound to be heard was a faint humming noise from the direction of Ms Wiz.

21

"That's better," said Caroline.

Brackenhurst's players were still waiting for the whistle to blow when Podge set off with the ball at his feet. He took two paces and booted it wildly. It was heading several feet wide of the Brackenhurst goal when, to everyone's astonishment, the ball changed direction and, as if it had a life of its own, flew into the back of the net.

For a moment, there was a stunned silence. Then Ms Wiz could be heard cheering on her team once more.

"What a shot!" she shouted. "Nice one, Podge!"

"Appalling behaviour," muttered Mrs Hicks.

From then on, the game altered completely. Not even in his wildest

dreams, when he had scored the winning goal for Spurs in the FA Cup Final, had Podge played so well.

Soon even Jack was shouting, "Give it to Podge! Give the ball to Podge!" while the Brackenhurst players were screaming, "Stop the fat one! Trip him, someone!"

But nobody could stop Podge. Playing as if he were under a spell, he scored three goals to give Class Five a great 3–2 victory.

After the game, the class gathered around Ms Wiz, shouting, cheering and singing songs.

"So much for her having her class under control," said Mrs Hicks. "They may win matches but Class Five are worse than ever with the new teacher."

Miss Gomaz had hurried over to Mr Gilbert.

"Just look at that, head teacher," she said, pointing to Class Five, who were now singing "Ms Wiz is magic!" at the top of their voices. "It's nothing short of anarchy."

But Mr Gilbert wasn't listening. He was still studying his new whistle and wondering why it hadn't worked.

CHAPTER THREE
AN EXTREMELY MATHEMATICAL OWL

"This is all very difficult," said Mr Gilbert, puffing nervously on his pipe. He was sitting in his study with Ms Wiz, who at this moment was looking at him with an annoying little smile on her face. "Very awkward. You see, Miss Wisdom – er, Ms Wiz – there have been, well, complaints."

"Goodness," said Ms Wiz brightly. "What on earth about?"

Mr Gilbert fumbled around with his pipe. Why *was* he feeling so nervous? Of course, he was always uneasy with women, but there were lots of women who were more frightening than Ms Wiz – Mrs Gilbert, for a start. The thought of his wife made the head teacher sit up in his armchair and try again.

"Firstly, there have been complaints about the way you look," he said, glancing at Ms Wiz. She was actually wearing black lipstick today.

"You find something wrong with the way I look?" asked Ms Wiz, who was beginning to be confused by this conversation.

"No, no," said Mr Gilbert, tapping his pipe on an ashtray. "I like … I mean, I don't … personally … Then," he said, quickly changing the subject, "there's what you teach. Your history lessons, for example."

"But Class Five loves history," said Ms Wiz. "We're doing the French Revolution at the moment."

"So I gather," said Mr Gilbert. "The

entire class was walking around the playground yesterday shouting, 'Behead the aristocrats!' I'm told that Jack was carrying a potato on the end of a sharp stick."

Ms Wiz laughed. "They're very keen," she said.

"Perhaps you could move on to some other part of history– *nice* history," said the head teacher. "1066, the Armada, King Alfred and the cakes."

"Oh no," said Ms Wiz. "We already have our next project."

"May I know what it is?" asked Mr Gilbert uneasily.

"Certainly," said Ms Wiz. "The Great Fire of London."

The head teacher gulped. Mrs Hicks and Miss Gomaz had been right. Ms Wiz spelt trouble.

"Perhaps," he said, "you could concentrate on some other subject for the time being."

"Of course," said Ms Wiz. "We'll try a spot of maths for a while."

Mr Gilbert smiled for the first time that morning.

"Perfect," he said.

Maths, he thought to himself after Ms Wiz had left his study. That couldn't cause trouble. Could it?

"Now, Class Five," said Ms Wiz that afternoon. "I'm going to test you on your nine times table – multiplication and division."

There was a groan around the classroom. Nobody liked the nine times table.

"And to help me," continued Ms Wiz, "I've brought my friend Archimedes." She reached inside her desk and brought out a large white owl. "Archie's what they call a bit of a number-cruncher. He loves his tables," she said, putting the owl on top of the blackboard.

"Cats, rats and now owls," muttered Katrina. "This place gets more like a zoo every day."

"Archie is a barn owl," said Ms Wiz, ignoring Katrina. "An extremely mathematical barn owl. Place the waste-paper basket beneath him please, Caroline."

"Why, Ms Wiz?" asked Caroline.

"Wait and see," said Ms Wiz.

Caroline put the waste-paper basket beneath Archie who was now looking around the classroom, blinking wisely.

"Now Podge," said Ms Wiz. "Tell Archie what five nines are."

"Forty-five," said Podge.

"Toowoo," went Archie.

"That means correct," said Ms Wiz. "Simon – nine nines."

"Eighty one," said Simon.

"Toowoo."

"Now Jack," said Ms Wiz. "Let's try division. A boy has 108 marbles He divides them between his nine friends. What does that make?"

"It makes him a wally for giving away all his marbles," said Jack.

Archie looked confused.

"Try again, Jack," said Ms Wiz patiently.

"Erm...eleven."

Class Five looked at Archie expectantly. Without a sound, the owl lifted its tail and did something very nasty into the waste-paper basket beneath him.

"Uuuuuuuurrrrgggghhhh, gross," said the children. "He's done a—"

"The correct word is guano," said Ms Wiz. "Jack?"

"Ten," said Jack.

Archie lifted his tail.

"Eight."

Archie did it again.

"How does he keep doing that?" asked Podge.

Ms Wiz shrugged. "He's well trained," she said.

"We'd better have another basket standing by," said Katrina. "Jack's never going to get it."

"He'd better," said Ms Wiz firmly.

"Every time Archie is obliged to do his...guano, it means fifty lines."

Jack groaned. "Um..."

Outside the door Mrs Hicks and Miss Gomaz were listening carefully.

They had left their classes with some reading work and were determined to catch the new teacher doing something wrong.

"Listen to that noise," said Miss Gomaz. "It's an absolute disgrace."

"Let's take a look through the window from the playground," said Mrs Hicks.

Moments later, the two teachers were watching in amazement as Jack struggled to give Archie the correct answer.

"There's a bird on the blackboard," whispered Miss Gomaz.

"It's...it's going to the lavatory," gasped Mrs Hicks. "In a bin. I can't believe my eyes."

They were just pressing their noses to the window-pane to get a closer look when Ms Wiz glanced up. Those at the front of the class could hear a slight hum coming from her direction.

"Miss Gomaz! Miss Gomaz!" said Mrs Hicks. "My nose! It's stuck to the glass!"

"Mine too!" cried Miss Gomaz, trying to pull back from the window-pane. "Ouch! That hurts!"

It was at that moment that the bell rang for afternoon break. Soon the teachers were surrounded by laughing children.

"Don't just stand there, you horrible children," screamed Mrs Hicks. "Get help quickly!"

"No need," said Ms Wiz, who had joined the children in the playground. She tapped the glass. Miss Gomaz and Mrs Hicks fell back, free at last.

"It must have been the frost," said Ms Wiz, with an odd little smile.

"Frost?" said Miss Gomaz, rubbing

her nose. "At this time of year? Don't talk daft."

"It's only September," said Mrs Hicks.

"Yes," said Ms Wiz. "What funny old weather we've been having, don't you think?"

CHAPTER FOUR

HERBERT TAKES A WRONG TURNING

It was during an art lesson that Class Five were first given an idea where Ms Wiz came from.

She had asked the children to draw an imaginary building. The project was called "The House of My Dreams".

Jack drew a house that looked like Wembley Stadium. It had a football pitch in the living room and all the walls were slanted like skateboard ramps.

Caroline drew the mansion that she would have when she became a film star. It had a huge lawn and swimming pool. In every room, there was a cocktail cabinet for drinks.

Podge drew Buckingham Palace made out of milk chocolate and fudge.

Katrina drew a strange, dark cottage in a wood. Cats with shining eyes stood guard on each side of the front door and bats flew in and out of its old thatched roof. She called it "Ms Wiz's Magic Cottage".

When Katrina finished the picture, Ms Wiz laughed. "It's lovely," she said, "but not at all like where I really live."

"Where *do* you live?" asked Katrina. The entire class grew quiet. Somehow no one had ever dared ask Ms Wiz about herself before.

"I live in a flat a long, long way away," said Ms Wiz. "At a place where almost certainly none of you have been. It's on the outskirts of town."

"Can we come and visit you during

the holidays?" asked Jack.

"During the holidays I'm doing other things," said Ms Wiz. "That's my job – to go wherever a little magic is needed. Wherever," she smiled, "things need shaking up a little."

"You've certainly shaken things up at St Barnabas," said Katrina. "Does that mean you'll be leaving us soon?"

Ms Wiz smiled. "Katrina, I'll only leave you when you no longer need me."

For a moment, there was silence in Class Five. Then Podge put up his hand.

"If you live so far away," he asked, "how do you get to school every day? Do you fly on your vacuum cleaner?"

"No," said Ms Wiz. "I come by bus."

*

If Ms Wiz was a little more serious than usual that afternoon, it was because she was thinking of the evening ahead of her. It was Parents' Evening.

Ms Wiz liked being with children. She didn't even mind being with teachers. But the idea of a whole evening spent in the company of parents made her feel tired already.

"I must remember to keep my spells under control," she said to herself as she waited for thefirst parent to arrive. "Adults aren't like children. Magic seems to upset them."

The door opened.

"I'm Harris," said a large man in a suit, who was the first parent to arrive. He shook Ms Wiz firmly by the hand. "Peter's dad. This," he nodded curtly towards a nervous-looking woman

standing a pace behind him, "is Mother."

Peter? Ms Wiz's mind raced. Who was Peter? Of course – that was Podge's real name.

"Pod – I mean Peter is doing well this term," she said, glancing at her notes.

"We're not happy," said Mr Harris firmly. "Isn't that right, Mother?"

43

"It is," said Mrs Harris. "We're not happy at all."

"The lad's gone strange on us," continued Mr Harris. "Always got his head in a book. Or talking about school. Asking us questions about this and that when his mother and I are trying to watch telly."

"Questions all the time," said Mrs Harris.

"Yak yak yak," said Mr Harris. "I'm a busy man. I work at the Town Hall. I want to relax of an evening, not answer questions from my own flesh and blood. That's your job."

Ms Wiz smiled. "Perhaps it's a good sign that he's interested in—"

"He's never been interested before. Tea, telly, bed was our way. Nothing wrong with that." Mr Harris leant forward angrily. "I've said to Mother and I'll say it to you. I smell a rat—" (for a horrible moment, Ms Wiz thought he had discovered Herbert, who was asleep up her sleeve) – "and when Cuthbert Harris smells a rat, heads will roll. Come on, Mother, I'm off."

Mr Harris stood up and, without another word, walked towards the door. Was it an accident that a banana skin had been left on the floor – or was it a touch of Ms Wiz magic after all?

"Woooaaaahhh!"

With a sickening crash, Mr Harris landed on the floor in a heap.

"Oh, Cuthbert!" said Mrs Harris. "Your best suit!"

Podge's father stood up, red-faced.

"Right! That's it!" he said as he dusted himself down."Town Hall's

going to hear of this. Heads will roll!"

Ms Wiz sighed as the door slammed behind Mr and Mrs Harris. Yes, she definitely preferred children to parents.

Ms Wiz was not often angry but when a few days after Parents' Evening, Mr Gilbert brought a School Inspector from the Town Hall into the classroom, there was an unusual sharpness in her tone when she addressed the class.

"Now sit up, Class Five," she said after the head teacher had left the School Inspector sitting at a little desk at the back of the class. "Remember we're being inspected today."

The School Inspector pursed his lips and made a note on the pad in front of him.

It was a quiet lesson without, of course, a hint of magic. Even Hecate the Cat remained hidden in Ms Wiz's bag.

Unfortunately nobody had told Herbert that Class Five was being inspected and Herbert, as luck would have it, decided on this particular moment to explore the classroom.

After a few minutes of the lesson, he had discovered a new tunnel. It was warm and dark, like a very inviting, old-fashioned chimney.

Who could blame him for wanting to explore it? Rats like chimneys. How was he to know that he was climbing up the left leg of the School Inspector's trousers?

At first the School Inspector twitched. Then he shifted nervously in

his seat. Then, as Herbert edged his
way past his knee and upwards, the
School Inspector stood up.

"Oh…ooh… ," he said, patting his
thigh."What the…oh…ah…" He
hopped around the classroom.

It was then that Herbert decided the
chimney was moving around rather
too much for comfort – and made for

the safety of the School Inspector's underpants.

"AAAARRRRRGGGGGHHHHH!"

The School Inspector tore at his belt, jumped out of his trousers and ran from the classroom.

Class Five watched in amazement as the half-naked figure sprinted across the playground, out of the school gates and down the road.

Relieved that the earthquake had passed, Herbert emerged nervously from the School Inspector's trousers on the classroom floor.

"Oh, Herbert," said Ms Wiz. "You've done it now."

CHAPTER FIVE
AN ABSOLUTE DISGRACE

Mr Gilbert was in a muddle. You might think that Mr Gilbert was always in a muddle, but this was the biggest muddle he had ever been in since he became head teacher of St Barnabas.

He was in such a muddle that his bald head had developed ugly red blotches. His attention would wander during lessons. He had even stopped picking his nose during Assembly.

"I'm on the horns of a dilemma," he told Mrs Gilbert one evening. "People keep telling me that Ms Wiz is a disaster. Miss Gomaz and Mrs Hicks say she's a troublemaker. The School Inspector says her classroom is a health hazard. Mr

Harris says heads will roll. They all want me to suspend her before the end-of-term prize giving next week."

"Suspend her then, Henry," said Mrs Gilbert. "What's the problem?"

"The problem is that the children of Class Five have won all the prizes this term. It's incredible. That sleepy Caroline has won the Art Prize. The A for Attitude Award for Good Behaviour has gone to Katrina of all people. Even the appalling Podge has won a Commendation for his story, 'The Enchanted Fudge Cake with a Thick Creamy Milk Chocolate Filling'. How on earth can I say, 'Well done everyone in Class Five and by the way I'm suspending your teacher'?"

"You'd better do what you think is best," said Mrs Gilbert. "But don't allow yourself to be bullied this time."

"Of course not," said Mr Gilbert. "You know where I stand on bullying."

"Let me guess," said Mrs Gilbert. "On the horns of a dilemma?"

"Precisely," said Mr Gilbert.

"Is it true that you're going to be suspended?" asked Katrina the next day in class. "Ever since the School Inspector lost his trousers, Mr Gilbert's been giving you some very funny looks."

"So have Miss Gomaz and Mrs Hicks," said Jack. "They look positively happy."

"My dad's smiling a lot," said Podge. "And that's never a good sign."

"Never you mind about me," said Ms Wiz. "I can look after myself."

"Yeah," said Simon. "You can magic 'em. That would show 'em."

"What have I always said? No unpleasant spells," said Ms Wiz.

"Oh, Ms,' said Podge. "Couldn't you just use a bit of magic – just one little spell on Mr Gilbert?"

"Maybe you could change him into a human being," suggested Jack.

There were cheers around the classroom. Ms Wiz held up her hands. Class Five were quiet.

"No," she said. "I refuse to listen to rumours. If the head teacher no longer requires my services, there's nothing to be done about it."

"Oh yes, there is," said Jack.

Which is how Class Five's Great Plan came into being.

*

End-of-term prizegiving was the most important event of the term for St Barnabas. It took place on the last day before the holidays and everybody was there.

On the platform in the School Hall sat Mr Gilbert, the School Inspector, all the teachers and the Lady Mayoress, a large, impressive woman who was wearing a large, impressive hat. In the audience were the children with their parents.

Mr Gilbert had just finished his end-of-term speech which, give or take a couple of pathetic jokes, was the same as every end-of-term speech he had made for the last ten years.

"Now," he said, "I would like to ask the Lady Mayoress—" Mr Gilbert gave a simpering little bow in her

direction "—to present the prizes. First, the Art Prize to Caroline Smith of Class Five."

There was polite applause as Caroline collected her prize.

"The Maths Prize has been won by Jack Beddows of Class Five."

Jack collected his prize, giving a modest wave to his supporters from the platform.

"The A for Attitude Award for Good Behaviour—" Mr Gilbert tried to keep the disbelief out of his voice, "to Katrina O'Brien of Class Five." Katrina actually gave a little curtsey to the Lady Mayoress as she was presented with her award.

"And Specially Commended for his essay, 'The Enchanted Fudge Cake with a Thick Creamy Milk Chocolate Filling' – Peter Harris of Class Five."

Podge climbed the steps to the platform. But instead of collecting his prize from the Lady Mayoress, he took the microphone from the astonished head teacher.

"Everyone in Class Five wants to thank Ms Wiz," he announced. "She's the best teacher we've ever had—"

"Give me that microphone, boy," said Mr Gilbert, chasing Podge around the stage.

"WE HOPE SHE NEVER EVER LEAVES!" shouted Podge. "Don't we, Class Five?"

At that moment, the children of Class Five stood up and started cheering. Several of them produced banners, reading "MS WIZ IS MAGIC" and "NO SACK FOR MS WIZ", which had been smuggled into the hall.

"You can stop that right now, Peter," said Podge's father, Mr Harris, advancing towards the platform."I'm going to give you a proper larrupping when you get home."

There was a humming sound from the back of the stage where Ms Wiz was sitting quietly.

Suddenly Mr Harris had turned into a strange pig-like animal.

"Goodness," said Miss Gomaz. "He's turned into a warthog."

"Surely not," said Mrs Hicks. "Warthogs don't have those funny little tusks. He looks more like a wild boar to me."

"Never mind that," shouted Mr Gilbert. "We have a full-scale riot on our baaa—" In a flash, there was a sheep standing in the head teacher's place.

By now the entire school was chanting, "We want Ms Wiz! We want Ms Wiz!"

Ms Wiz stood up and Podge gave her the microphone.

"I think," she said firmly, "that we should continue Prizegiving in half an hour. I'd like to see Class Five in their classroom now, please."

She made her way through the audience, which was now silent.

"Phone the police, Miss Gomaz," hissed Mrs Hicks.

Ms Wiz glanced over her shoulder. Suddenly where Miss Gomaz and Mrs Hicks had been standing, there were two grey geese, making a furious gobbling noise.

*

"That was very kind of you, Class Five," said Ms Wiz, when all the children had gathered in the classroom. "But the fact is, I'm leaving St Barnabas anyway."

There was silence in the classroom.

"Why?" asked Katrina eventually.

"After all that," muttered Podge.

"I go where magic is needed," said Ms Wiz. "Where things need livening up. Today you've proved that you no longer need me. You're the best class in the school."

"We won't be, without you," said Caroline.

"Yes, you will," said Ms Wiz. "Wait and see."

"We'll miss you," said Jack, serious for once.

"No, you won't because..."

The class looked expectantly at Ms Wiz. Caroline managed to stop sniffling at the back of the class.

"…because I'll be back," said Ms Wiz.

"When?"

"Where?"

"Next term?"

Ms Wiz held up her hands.

"I'll come back and see each one of you," she said with a smile. "When you least expect it, when you need a spot of Ms Wiz in your life, I'll be there."

"Every one of us?" asked Simon.

"Every one of you," said Ms Wiz. "And I'll bring Hecate the Cat and Herbert."

Ms Wiz gathered up her bag. She swung her leg over her vacuum cleaner, like a cowboy about to ride out of town on his horse.

"Go back to the School Hall and finish prizegiving," she said. "You'll find everything's back to normal."

Ms Wiz hovered in mid-air by the classroom window.

"See you soon, Class Five," she said and flew off across the playground and over the School Hall.

"Oh no," said Jack as the class filed back into the hall. "Look who Ms Wiz has forgotten."

On the platform beside Mr Gilbert, the School Inspector and the Lady Mayoress, who were looking as if nothing strange had happened at all, stood two grey geese.

"She'll *have* to come back now," said Katrina.

"No unpleasant spells," said Podge.

They heard a familiar hum from outside the hall.

"Gobble gobble gobble – absolute disgrace," said Miss Gomaz.

Jack sighed.

"I think I preferred them as geese," he said.

Ms Wiz

LOVES DRACULA

This book is dedicated to
all the children who have written
to me about MsWiz.

Acknowledgements

I would like to thank Salvatore Genco,
Andrea Kaizer and Darren Wade of
Eastfield Primary School, Enfield,
whose own Ms Wiz story was the
original inspiration for this book,
and all the pupils of Mowbray County
Junior School, South Shields, for their
helpful comments on the
story itself.

CHAPTER ONE

A LOAD OF PARENTS GETTING DRUNK

It was the end of the last day of autumn term at St Barnabas School. Children were running across the playground to be met by their parents at the school gate. From the gym nearby could be heard the sound of a radio playing. Tonight was the night of the Christmas fancy-dress dance held by the PTA, and some of the teachers were putting up the decorations.

With their satchels slung over their shoulders, Jack Beddows and Lizzie Thompson stood at the doorway of the gym and watched as Class Five's teacher, Mr Bailey, climbed a stepladder to attach balloons to the wall bars.

"Call themselves the Parent Teacher Association," said Jack. "All they want to do is prance about in fancy dress."

Lizzie smiled. "Miss Gomaz told Class Four that she was going as Teddy Edward. There's a rumour that Mr Gilbert's hired a Superman costume."

"Is it a bird? Is it a plane?" said Jack in his favourite American accent. "No, it's the head teacher of St Barnabas School in a silly suit."

"I wonder what Mr Bailey's going as," whispered Lizzie.

"A ghost, probably," said Jack. "He'd look all right with a sheet over his head."

As if he had heard their conversation, Mr Bailey glanced over and saw the two children standing in the doorway. "Off you go, you two," he called out. "It's the grown-ups' time now."

"Bye, sir," Jack called out. "Don't forget to dance with Teddy Edward."

It was getting dark as Jack and Lizzie made their way across the school playground and out of the gate towards Lizzie's house where Jack was staying that night.

"I know it's only a stupid fancy-dress dance but I really wish we were going," Jack said. "I'd give anything to see Mr Gilbert as the Man of Steel."

"And we've got Helen from next door babysitting," said Lizzie gloomily. "She's really strict about when we go to bed."

"If only we had—" Jack had been just about to say, "If only we had Ms Wiz as a babysitter," when he saw a familiar figure sitting on a wall across the road from the school. She was wearing a long overcoat and a woolly hat, but that dark hair was unmistakable. "Look who it is," he said.

"I don't believe it," said Lizzie. "She hasn't visited us for ages."

"Ms Wiz!" Jack shouted as they ran towards a zebra crossing nearby, but the figure continued to look down at the pavement, deep in thought.

"She doesn't look very happy," murmured Lizzie as they approached. "Perhaps she's lost her magic."

"Yo, Ms Wiz," Jack called out.

Ms Wiz looked up, as if awakening from a daydream. "Hi, Jack," she smiled. "Hi, Lizzie."

"We were just talking about you," said Jack. "I'm staying with Lizzie tonight and we need a babysitter."

"Yeah, it's unfair," said Lizzie. "My mum and Jack's parents are going to the PTA fancy-dress dance and we have to stay at home with the world's strictest babysitter."

"Fancy dress?" Suddenly Ms Wiz looked interested. "That sounds fun."

"Nah, you'd hate it," said Jack. "It's just a load of parents getting drunk and dancing with teachers to really old sixties songs."

"Great." Ms Wiz jumped down off the wall. "Where can I get a ticket?"

Mrs Thompson was in a bad mood. Lizzie and Jack had promised not to be late back from school, and they were. The shop where she had hired a nurse's uniform for tonight's dance had promised it would fit her, and it didn't. She was looking at herself in the hall mirror when the bell rang.

"Glad you could make it," she said, opening the door to Lizzie and Jack.

Lizzie looked at her mother in the nurse's uniform. "Er, you look great, Mum," she said eventually.

"Yeah, dig Florence Nightingale," said Jack in a serious attempt at politeness.

"I look ridiculous," moaned Mrs Thompson. "I'm all ... bulgy."

From the darkness behind Jack and Lizzie could be heard a faint humming sound.

"What's happening?" Mrs Thompson looked down at her uniform which seemed to be slowly expanding. After a few seconds, the material stopped moving. It was now a perfect fit.

"Is that any better?" asked Ms Wiz, stepping out of the shadows.

"This is Ms Wiz," said Lizzie. "You remember the Paranormal Operative

who used to visit Class Five? Well, she's back and, as you can see, her magic's still working."

"Paranormal Operative? Magic?" Mrs Thompson looked from the nurse's uniform to Ms Wiz. "The costume won't shrink back at the wrong moment, will it?" she asked nervously. "I don't want to go all bulgy again just when I'm dancing with Mr Gilbert."

Ms Wiz laughed. "No," she said. "Anyway, I'll be there to make sure the spell keeps working."

"Will you?" Mrs Thompson looked surprised.

"Ms Wiz wants to go to the dance," Lizzie explained.

"Weren't you banned once from St Barnabas?" asked Mrs Thompson.

"Something about sending a class on a field trip to the other side of the world?"

Ms Wiz shrugged. "It was a long time ago. Anyway, no one will recognize me in fancy dress."

"I'm not sure." Mrs Thompson frowned as she turned towards the kitchen. "Will you promise not to do any of your spells?" she asked.

"Trust me," said Ms Wiz.

"Oh, all right," said Mrs Thompson. "You can change in my room upstairs."

"But what will you change into?" Lizzie asked.

Ms Wiz smiled. "I'll think of something," she said.

"There's one thing I don't understand," said Jack, after Ms Wiz had gone to change. "Whenever Ms Wiz comes to see us, she tells us that she goes where magic is needed."

"That's true," said Lizzie. "There's always a problem that needs solving when she turns up."

"So who is it who needs the magic now?" asked Jack. There was silence in the kitchen as the three of them thought about this.

"Perhaps it's Ms Wiz herself who needs the magic," said Mrs Thompson eventually.

"Ms Wiz need magic?" Jack laughed. "Never."

"She might be lonely," said Mrs Thompson. "That would explain why she's so keen on going to the dance."

"Maybe she's looking for a boyfriend," said Lizzie.

Jack laughed. "Don't be ridiculous," he said. "Ms Wiz isn't like that – anyway she's got Herbert the rat for company."

"A rat's not quite the same as a boyfriend," said Lizzie.

"Hmm," said Mrs Thompson. "No comment."

There was a rustling sound from the stairs. A dark, wild-haired witch dressed in stylish black off-the-shoulder rags, her green eyes sparkling, made her way slowly down the stairs.

"How do I look?" asked Ms Wiz.

CHAPTER TWO
STRANGERS IN THE NIGHT

Before Dracula arrived, it had been a
PTA dance like any other PTA dance.
There was soggy quiche. There was
wine which even Mrs Hicks, who
could drink almost anything, had
difficulty in swallowing. One of the
dads had already hurt his back doing
the twist. In spite of all Mr Bailey's
efforts, the gym didn't really look
like a disco – it looked like a gym
with a few balloons hanging from the
walls.

Ms Wiz stood with Lizzie's mother
near the Christmas tree. She wanted to
dance but the fathers seemed to be too
nervous to speak to her.

"I think they recognize me," she whispered to Mrs Thompson. "They're worried I'll bewitch them or something."

Mrs Thompson glanced at Ms Wiz. "The trouble is we're not used to such glamorous witches at St Barnabas," she said. "We have this idea that a witch should be an old girl with a hunchback, long dirty fingernails, and a drip on the end of her crooked nose."

"How very old-fashioned," sighed Ms Wiz, smiling at a small figure in a strange costume who was now approaching them.

"Hullo, I'm the head teacher," said Mr Gilbert, shaking Ms Wiz's hand. He gave a nervous little laugh. "Except tonight I'm Superman."

"Ah yes," said Mz Wiz, who had been wondering why he was wearing

blue pyjamas and a little red cape.
"Pleased to meet you, Superman."

"Now, I can't help feeling we've met somewhere before," said Mr Gilbert.

"I don't think so," said Ms Wiz quickly. "My name's—"

It was at that precise moment that the music stopped and the lights went out.

There were groans from around the gym. "Not *another* power cut," said a voice in the darkness. "That's the third time the electricity's gone off this week."

Someone standing by the doorway lit a match. The door behind him opened to reveal a tall, dark figure with glittering eyes. Two long incisor teeth protruded slightly over his lower lip.

"Got a torch, Count Dracula?" laughed one of the parents.

The figure in black said nothing.

"Typical," laughed Lizzie's mother, as Mr Gilbert hurried away to find some candles. "Something like this always happens at the PTA dance. But at least it saved you from having to dance with Superman."

"Mmm?" Ms Wiz was staring across the room.

"That man's got the heaviest feet—" Mrs Thompson realized that Ms Wiz was no longer listening to her. "Have you seen someone you know?"

A hint of colour had come to Ms Wiz's cheeks. "I think I've just seen the vampire of my dreams," she said.

Lizzie wasn't tired. Nor was Jack. They sat in Lizzie's room listening to the television downstairs and wondering what was happening at the PTA dance.

"My mum says that when you can't sleep, you should get up and walk around a bit," said Lizzie.

Jack thought about this for a moment. "Perhaps we could walk down the road to St Barnabas. The fresh air would do us good. We could take a look at the dance through the window of the gym."

"What about Helen, downstairs?" Lizzie whispered.

"We'll only be gone a few minutes. She's probably asleep in front of the telly."

Without another word, the two children dressed.

"This is bad," muttered Lizzie as, a few minutes later, they stood at the top of the stairs. "My mum'll kill me if she sees us."

They crept downstairs, silently lifted the spare front door key off a hook in the hall and let themselves out of the house into the dark night.

It had been one of the strangest dances she had ever been to, Lizzie's mother thought as she danced with Mr Harris. First of all, when the electricity had come back on, there had been an odd humming noise from the direction of Ms Wiz. Suddenly the lights in the gym had dimmed, giving it a soft, romantic glow.

"That's better," Ms Wiz had said.

Without another word, she had walked across the room and had introduced herself to Dracula.

Then there was the music. Normally it was loud and fast at the PTA dance but, when Ms Wiz had first walked onto the dance floor with Dracula, she had glanced at the cassette player, there had been another humming noise – and, from then on, the only music the machine would play was slow, smoochy Frank Sinatra songs, to which Ms Wiz and Dracula danced all evening.

Not that the music made any difference to Mr Harris, Mrs Thompson sighed to herself. As usual, he was pushing her around the dance floor like a removal man delivering a cupboard on his last shift. Over his shoulder, Mrs Thompson smiled as she saw Dracula and Ms Wiz dancing slowly in one of the darker corners.

"It's all very strange indeed," she murmured.

"What's that, love?" Mr Harris barked in her ear.

"Um, it's strange how well you dance," said Mrs Thompson quickly.

"Oh yes, I like a good old stomp," said Mr Harris, treading hard on her right toe.

As the song ended, Ms Wiz and Dracula slipped out of the gym and into the playground.

"I'd better be going home now," said Dracula in a deep, silky voice.

"Of course," Ms Wiz smiled cheerfully. "The last train for Transylvania must be leaving soon."

"Perhaps we could, you know…"
Dracula seemed to be lost for words.
"D'you fancy going to the cinema
some time?"

Ms Wiz laughed. "Afternoon show, I
suppose. You must be busy at night."

"Busy?"

"Night shift. All that flying about
with the other vampires."

"Yes, of course." Dracula sighed. "It
does keep me busy."

For a moment, there was an awkward
silence in the playground, except for the
sound of "Strangers in the Night"
drifting across from the gym.

"Well," said Ms Wiz softly. "It's
been a great pleasure." She shook
Dracula's hand and turned away.

"What did you say your name
was?" Dracula called out.

"Ms Wiz. But you can call me Dolores."

"Can I telephone you?"

Ms Wiz hesitated. "I'm not on the telephone, I'm afraid," she said. "But I suppose you could leave a message for me with Lizzie's mother, Mrs Thompson." She waved and walked into the gym.

"Who's Lizzie? Who's Mrs Thompson?" murmured Dracula to himself. "Oh, I'll never see that beautiful witch again." He took a handkerchief out of his top pocket and blew his nose. Then, slowly and sadly, he walked out of the school gates and down the road.

*

"Talk about embarrassing," said Jack, emerging from the shadows nearby. "For one moment, I thought they were going to kiss or something gross like that."

"They couldn't," said Lizzie. "His teeth would get in the way, wouldn't they?" Glancing down, she noticed a small white card on the ground. "He dropped something," she said, picking it up. "It says 'College of National Assessment'. Then there's an address. Maybe he wasn't Dracula after all."

"Of course he was," said Jack. "I mean, he wouldn't go around with cards saying 'DRACULA – VAMPIRE AND BLOODSUCKING NEEDS – ESTIMATES FREE', would he? That card's just to throw people off his track."

Lizzie was walking towards the school gate. "He seemed a bit shy for a vampire," she said.

"That was a vampire, all right," said Jack. "Can you imagine Ms Wiz dancing the night away with just an ordinary bloke in a silly fancy dress?"

"I don't know," said Lizzie. "I don't seem to know anything about Ms Wiz any more."

CHAPTER THREE

A GORGEOUS, HUNKY LORD OF THE UNDEAD

A low moaning sound could be heard coming from the kitchen when Lizzie and Jack came down to breakfast the following morning.

"Oh no," Lizzie sighed. Mrs Thompson was sitting at the kitchen table, her head in her hands, staring into a cup of coffee.

"Your mum looks really ill," whispered Jack.

"It's what's called a hangover," said Lizzie, speaking as loudly as before. "Every year Mum goes to the PTA dance and every year she has this special PTA dance hangover from

drinking too much."

"Someone must have put something in the wine, I only had two glasses," muttered Mrs Thompson, as she looked up at the children with small, bloodshot eyes.

"It's called alcohol, Mum," said Lizzie.

"Where's Ms Wiz?" asked Jack, anxious to change the subject.

"Flew home after the dance," said Mrs Thompson. She sipped at her coffee. "I think she lost her heart to Dracula."

"Her heart? Ugh, you mean he just took it?" said Jack. "Didn't it make a mess on the dance floor?"

Mrs Thompson laughed, then winced.

"No jokes," she begged. "Don't make me laugh."

"It wasn't really Dracula, was it?" asked Lizzie, thinking of the card she had picked up in the playground.

"No one knew who he was." Mrs Thompson stood up slowly. "Wasn't a parent, wasn't a teacher. Maybe Ms Wiz thought the PTA dance was a Bring Your Own Vampire party."

The front doorbell rang loudly.

"I wonder who that could be," said Lizzie.

Mrs Thompson was tottering towards the stairs. "Tell them to go away. I'm off back to bed," she muttered, as Jack and Lizzie ran to the front door.

An extraordinary sight greeted their eyes. Ms Wiz, wearing a pink T-shirt covered with purple hearts, was hovering six inches above the ground. A cloud of beautiful yellow butterflies flitted around her head.

"Jack! Lizzie!" she exclaimed in a strange, fluting voice. "I was passing by and I just wanted to tell you that it's an absolutely *wonderful* morning."

Lizzie held the front door open as Ms Wiz floated into the house, followed by the yellow butterflies.

"Are you feeling all right, Ms Wiz?" Jack asked. "Why aren't your feet on the ground? You look all ... weird."

"Weird? *Moi?*" Ms Wiz smiled dreamily. "I've never felt better in my life. I suppose there aren't any—" she fluttered her eyelashes "—messages for me."

"What sort of messages?" asked Lizzie.

"You know, little notes written in blood which have been popped through the letterbox. Maybe a present – a dead bat perhaps or—"

"From Dracula, you mean," said Jack.

"Dracula?" Ms Wiz smiled innocently.

"Everybody knows about you and Dracula," said Lizzie. "You were the talk of the PTA dance."

Ms Wiz flew around the hall, singing out, "My head's in a spin, my heart's on fire, I've fallen in love with a bloodsucking vampire."

"Er, Ms Wiz—" said Jack.

"We'll stay together, we'll never part, my love for Drax is like a stake through my heart."

"Ms Wiz, I think—" said Lizzie, trying to interrupt.

"Blood is red, veins are blue, his fangs are pearly and—"

"Ms Wiz!" shouted Jack. "Stop floating about the hall spouting poetry, and just think about this. You cannot fall in love with a vampire."

Ms Wiz paused mid-flight. "Why not?" she smiled. "This is the real thing at last."

"Yes, but is *he* a real thing?" asked Lizzie. "After all, you did meet him at a fancy dress dance. Maybe he's not a real vampire."

"Of course he is," Ms Wiz smiled.

"I'd know a vampire anywhere. Those cute, long nails. Those dark, sweet, evil eyes."

"All right, let's say he is Dracula," said Jack. "He's not exactly going to be a perfect boyfriend, is he? I mean, think of all that bloodsucking. After a few nights out with him, your neck would be like a pincushion."

Ms Wiz frowned and touched her neck nervously. Then she shrugged. "Oh, fiddle-di-dee," she said. "What's a bit of bloodsucking between friends?"

"Then there's the garlic," said Lizzie. "When you go out to a restaurant, you'll always have to worry about what's in the meal. Vampires hate garlic."

"The course of love never did run smooth," smiled Ms Wiz. "Even with a gorgeous, hunky Lord of the Undead."

"And think of Class Five," said Jack desperately. "Can you imagine how upset they'll be when they hear you're dating a vampire?"

"That's no problem," said Ms Wiz. "You can all come and visit us in Count Dracula's dark, crumbling castle in Transylvania."

Lizzie reached into the back pocket of her jeans. She didn't want to upset Ms Wiz but it was time for a bit of reality. "He doesn't actually live in Transylvania," she said. "He dropped his card in the playground. The Lord of the Undead seems to live at 43, Addison Gardens."

"The neighbours must be pleased," muttered Jack.

For the first time, Ms Wiz floated down to earth. "You ... you have the address of my beloved?" she asked faintly. "We must go there right now."

"Promise you won't be disappointed?" asked Lizzie.

"Take me to my fanged one," said Ms Wiz, hovering by the front door.

Lizzie looked at Jack, who shrugged. "Why not?" he said.

"Oh well, it's only five minutes away," sighed Lizzie. Picking up her coat, she called up the stairs, "Mum, we're just going down the road with Ms Wiz on a love quest for a bloodsucking vampire, all right?"

"Mmmm," moaned Mrs Thompson.

43, Addison Gardens was a block of flats. Beside the door were six doorbells with names beside them. None of them was that of Count Dracula.

"It must be the top flat," said Ms Wiz. "Vampires are like bats – they live under the roof."

"We can't just ring the top bell and ask if Dracula's at home," said Lizzie.

"I'll fly up and spy through the window," suggested Ms Wiz.

While they were talking, Jack had crept to a nearby window. Now he beckoned them over urgently.

Through the window could be seen a small room. A long, black cloak had been thrown over a chair near the window. Pacing backwards and forwards was a tall, good-looking man with dark hair and glasses. Now and then, he would pause to look at an object on a table nearby. They were a set of false vampire's fangs.

"I recognize him," whispered Lizzie. "It's the new school inspector."

"You're right," said Jack. "What was his name? Mr Arnold – that was it. He visited us at the beginning of term."

"A school inspector?" said Ms Wiz.

"I'm afraid so." Lizzie looked at Ms Wiz sympathetically. "He wasn't Dracula after all."

"Look on the bright side," said Jack. "There'll be other vampires."

A smile had appeared once more on Ms Wiz's face. She floated off the ground, singing out, "Ms Wiz was blind, you were right to correct her, her heart belongs to a school inspector."

"I don't believe it," said Jack.

CHAPTER FOUR
IT'S MAGIC OR ME

Ever since Lizzie's father had left home when she was five, Lizzie had been really close to her mother. She liked seeing her father at weekends but, when it came to the real problems in her life, there was only one person she could talk to.

"We've got a crisis, Mum," she said as they sat watching television together a few days later. "People have been seeing Ms Wiz and Mr Arnold everywhere. At the cinema. Feeding the ducks in the park. Podge swears he saw them walking down the High Street holding hands."

"Nice." Mrs Thompson was half-

listening, her eyes on the screen. "I'm so glad he wasn't a real vampire."

"But it's not right for Ms Wiz to be hanging around the cinema and the park. It's so...normal."

"I told you she was lonely," said Mrs Thompson. "Just because she does a bit of magic now and then, it doesn't mean she's not interested in having a boyfriend."

"But you're not interested in having a boyfriend," said Lizzie.

"That's because I was married to your father," said Mrs Thompson, pursing her lips as if she could say more but didn't want to. "He cured me of men."

"There's an idea," said Lizzie. "Perhaps I could introduce Dad to Ms Wiz on our next weekend together. Maybe he'd cure her too."

Mrs Thompson laughed. "He couldn't handle a normal person, let alone a paranormal operative with rats, china cats and weird spells." She frowned. "I wonder if Mr Arnold knows about all that."

Lizzie thought about this for a moment. Then she leapt to her feet. "Mum, you're a genius," she said, making for the door.

"Where are you going?" asked Mrs Thompson.

"I'm phoning Jack," Lizzie called over her shoulder. "I've just thought of a solution to our crisis."

Brian Arnold walked down the High Street, which was packed with Christmas shoppers. Smiling, he whistled softly to himself. He didn't think he had ever been so happy in his life.

It had been a matter of sheer luck that he had gone to the St Barnabas dance – he had only accepted Mr Gilbert's invitation out of politeness. Yet there, as if by magic, he had met the most beautiful woman in the world.

"Yes, it really was as if by magic,"

he had said to Ms Wiz on their first date together two days after the dance.

"It wasn't magic, it was life," Ms Wiz had replied with the merest hint of irritation in her voice. "Magic had nothing to do with it." Mr Arnold had never discovered why the word "magic" seemed to upset her so much.

There was another wonderful thing. Mr Arnold loved children – that was why he had become a school inspector – but, until recently, he had rarely been friends with them outside school hours. Ever since he had met Ms Wiz, he always seemed to be meeting children from Class Five. It was almost as if they were following him.

In fact, he was seeing some children this very afternoon. Jack and Lizzie had invited him out for a Christmas hamburger at the Big Burger Bar on the High Street. Ms Wiz had promised to meet them there.

"A lovely girlfriend. Children offering me a Christmas hamburger." Mr Arnold smiled to himself as he opened the door to the Big Burger Bar. "What a lucky man I am."

Jack and Lizzie were already sipping cokes at a corner table.

"This was an excellent idea," he said as he took his seat.

"Mum said we could buy you burgers as a sort of Christmas present," smiled Lizzie.

"Very decent of you," said Mr Arnold. "I wonder where Dolores has got to."

"Dolores?" Jack frowned. "Oh, you mean Ms Wiz. She'll probably fly in on her vacuum cleaner – just like she did

when we first met her at St Barnabas."

"Vacuum cleaner?" The school inspector smiled politely. "How exactly can someone fly on a vacuum cleaner?"

"The same way as someone can turn Podge's father into a warthog. Or Mr Gilbert into a sheep," said Jack. "If that someone happens to have magic powers, like Ms Wiz has."

"Excuse me, children—" Mr Arnold cleared his throat nervously. "Are you

telling me that Dolores – er, Ms Wiz –
is... not quite as other women?"

"Of course she's not," said Jack.
"You mean she never told you? She
calls herself a paranormal operative.
It's a sort of modern witch." He pulled
a small bottle from his pocket. "This
little bottle had my appendix in it after
I had an operation at the hospital –
that is, until Mr Bailey, my teacher, ate
it, thanks to a bit of Ms Wiz magic."

"And she's got this rat she keeps
under her shirt," said Lizzie. "It ran
up the leg of the last school inspector's
trousers during a lesson."

Mr Arnold nodded slowly. "So that
was why Mr Smith left the job in such
a hurry. When I was given his job, I
was told that he had problems with
his nerves."

"Hi, everyone."

Lizzie, Jack and Mr Arnold turned to see Ms Wiz, waving as she made her way across the restaurant towards them.

"What's the matter?" she said, as she arrived. "You all look as if you've seen a ghost."

"Not a ghost," said Mr Arnold grimly. "But a paranormal operative."

"Ah." Ms Wiz sat down slowly. "You've heard."

"Jack and Lizzie have been telling me all about your spells."

"Thanks, Jack. Thanks, Lizzie." Ms Wiz picked up the menu, as if nothing unusual had happened. "Now, I wonder if they have anything vegetarian here," she said.

"Dolores, I must ask you a question." Mr Arnold sat forward in his seat. "Do you or do you not keep a magic rat in your underwear?"

A faint humming sound came from across the table. "Oh look!" Ms Wiz pointed behind them. "Flying hamburgers!" There were gasps from the diners as hamburgers floated off their plates to swoop around the restaurant, splashing relish, mayonnaise and tomato sauce everywhere. "Isn't that strange, Brian?"

But Mr Arnold ignored the hamburgers. "You're just making it worse by trying to put me off with some sort of conjuring trick," he said. "Tell me about the rat. Do you—?"

A crash of plates, followed by the thud of bodies hitting the ground, interrupted him. "That's odd, Brian," said Ms Wiz desperately. "The floor of

the restaurant has been changed into an ice rink. Those poor waiters are falling all over the place."

"The rat, Dolores," said Mr Arnold.

As the humming noise died down, the flying hamburgers settled back onto their plates and the waiters picked themselves up off the floor. Ms Wiz sighed and reached inside her T-shirt, pulling out a small, brown rat which she put on the table. "Tell him, Herbert," she said.

"It's very simple," said the rat, in a squeaky but well-educated voice. "My name is Herbert and I am indeed a magic rat. I would like to take this opportunity to apologize profusely for running up your former colleague's trousers."

There was a scream from a nearby

table. "A rat!" With a trembling hand, a woman pointed to Herbert. "And it's talking!"

"Yeah, yeah!" said Herbert, glancing casually in her direction. "Now, as I was saying—"

Mr Arnold had heard enough. He pushed back his chair and stood up. "That's it, Dolores," he said to Ms Wiz. "Call me old-fashioned but I'm not going out with someone who makes hamburgers fly off plates and goes around with talking rats in her undergarments." He backed towards the door. "You have to choose, Dolores – it's magic or me." Without another word, he blundered out of the door and into the street outside.

"Whoops," said Jack.

"I'm sorry, Ms Wiz." Lizzie laid a

hand on Ms Wiz's arm. "We shouldn't have told him about your magic."

"Never mind." Ms Wiz smiled bravely. "He had to find out some time." She sighed. "Oh well, there goes my Christmas Day with Mr Arnold." She picked up Herbert and slipped him back under her T-shirt.

"Why don't you come round to us?" asked Lizzie. "Mum and I would love to see you."

"And I could bring your friends from Class Five around in the afternoon," said Jack.

Ms Wiz was staring out of the window, as if looking for Mr Arnold. "That would be lovely," she said quietly.

CHAPTER FIVE
THE LAST SPELL OF CHRISTMAS

"A party for Ms Wiz this afternoon? All her friends from Class Five there?" said Podge's father Mr Harris on Christmas morning. "No way. Yuletide is a time for families, not weird, green-eyed women with magic powers."

"But, Dad," Podge pleaded. "Everyone's going to be there. For Class Five, Ms Wiz *is* family. Lizzie and Jack say she needs cheering up."

"She's always been trouble, Ms Who'sit," said Mr Harris. "What do you think, Mother?"

Mrs Harris placed a hand on Podge's shoulders. "I think that, if you don't let

123

him go, you'll be cooking your own turkey," she said firmly.

"Typical," grumbled Mr Harris. "Not even Christmas is safe from that woman."

Ms Wiz sat at the head of Mrs Thompson's table, her pale face illuminated by the Christmas tree nearby. "This is the best Christmas I've ever had," she said quietly. "Before we have tea, I'd just like to thank Lizzie and Mrs Thompson for inviting me for Christmas dinner and to all my friends in Class Five for coming to tea."

She looked around the table at the smiling faces of Lizzie, Jack, Podge, Caroline, Katrina, Carl and Nabila. "Seeing you all again has reminded

me of all the strange adventures we've had together."

"But we'll be having more adventures in the future, won't we, Ms Wiz?" asked Katrina.

Before Ms Wiz could answer, Mrs Thompson appeared at the doorway, carrying a large cake, which she put down carefully in the middle of the table. Written in green on the cake's white icing were the words, "HAPPY CHRISTMAS, Ms WIZ."

"I don't know how to thank you," said Ms Wiz. "How about a trick?" suggested Jack. "Yeah," the children agreed. "Trick! Trick! Trick!" they chanted.

Ms Wiz held up her hands. "I have an announcement to make," she said when silence had returned to the room. "After my recent … experiences with a certain school inspector, I've decided I want to lead a more normal life. Of course, that … experience is over, but all the same I plan to get a flat somewhere around here. I'll be applying for a job as a teacher."

"Great," said Carl. "We can have magic every day."

"Well, no." Ms Wiz smiled. "The only way that I can become part of the normal world is to agree to give up magic."

There was a stunned silence.

"How exactly do you give up magic?" Nabila asked shyly. "Is there a strange ceremony with lots of Latin and chanting?"

Ms Wiz laughed. "All I have to do is—"

She was interrupted by the sound of three loud knocks coming from the hall.

Mrs Thompson frowned. "Who on earth could that be?" she said. There was silence as she walked out of the room to open the front door – followed by a blood-curdling scream.

The children stared at the sitting room door. First they saw a shadow, then a dark, cloaked figure filled the doorway, its fangs shining in the gloom.

"Yes." The voice coming from the figure was like ghostly wind rustling the leaves of an ancient oak tree. "I am Dracula." He moved slowly towards the table. "I have heard that the brotherhood of vampires has been

mocked by one pretending to be the Lord of the Undead. Is this true?"

Nobody answered.

"Those who have laughed at the Undead shall pay a terrible price," the stranger continued.

"Is that you, M-M-Mr Arnold?" Lizzie managed to say at last.

It was as if Dracula had heard nothing. "First to pay—" the dark figure fixed its eyes upon Ms Wiz, " — will be the woman who actually danced with the pretender."

Ms Wiz stood up slowly. "What do you want of me?" she asked quietly.

"All I want—" Dracula sneered evilly as he moved more closely. "All I want—"

"Get some garlic from the kitchen, Mum," Lizzie said to Mrs Thompson. "We need to save Ms Wiz before it's too late."

"All I want...for Christmas is my two front teeth." With a pale hand, Dracula reached up to his mouth and removed his fangs. "Happy Christmas, Dolores," he said.

"Eh?" muttered Jack. "What's going on?"

Dracula took off his cloak, smiled, and put on a pair of glasses.

"I don't believe it," said Lizzie. "It was Mr Arnold all the time."

"A vampire for Christmas," said Ms Wiz, her eyes sparkling. "Just what I always wanted."

"Honestly," said Mrs Thompson. "Calls himself a school inspector and he comes round on Christmas Day to scare the living daylights out of children. This man's almost as odd as Ms Wiz."

"It's why we get on so well," said Ms Wiz.

"I just had to say I'm sorry about walking out of the Big Burger Bar," said Mr Arnold. "All those spells took me by surprise."

"Hey," said Caroline. "Now Mr

Arnold's back, you won't have to give up your magic."

As if in reply, a faint humming sound filled the room. The lights lifted off the Christmas tree, hovered in the air, then made an archway over Ms Wiz.

"Listen to me, Class Five," she said, stretching her arms out in front of her. "On this Christmas Day, we are faced with a choice. If you wish me to live in your neighbourhood so that you can see me every day, I shall have to retire from being a paranormal operative. You have to decide whether you like me for my magic or for myself."

"For yourself," said the children.

"But the magic helps," muttered Jack.

Ms Wiz reached into her coloured

canvas bag that was nearby. She took out Hecate, her enchanted china cat, and placed it on the table. "As from now, this is but a normal china cat," she said.

She reached into her T-shirt and took out her magic rat Herbert. She gave him to Jack.

"That," she said as Herbert ran up Jack's arm to perch on his shoulder, "is now but an ordinary pet rat."

"And I—" The humming noise faded. The lights returned slowly to the Christmas tree. "As from today, I'll just be Dolores Wisdom. Only in real emergencies will I become Ms Wiz again." She smiled, first at Mr Arnold, who stood beside her, and then at the children. "Any questions?"

There was silence.

"Just one," said Podge at last. "Are we ever going to eat that Christmas cake?"

Laughing, Mrs Thompson passed Ms Wiz a knife. Everyone clapped as she cut the first slice.

"I say," a voice whispered in Jack's ear. "I'd be most awfully grateful if you slipped us a piece of that cake." It was Herbert the rat.

"Er, Ms Wiz," said Jack quietly. "I think the magic is still—"

Ms Wiz looked up and winked. "Still what, Jack?"

"Er, nothing, Dolores," said Jack.